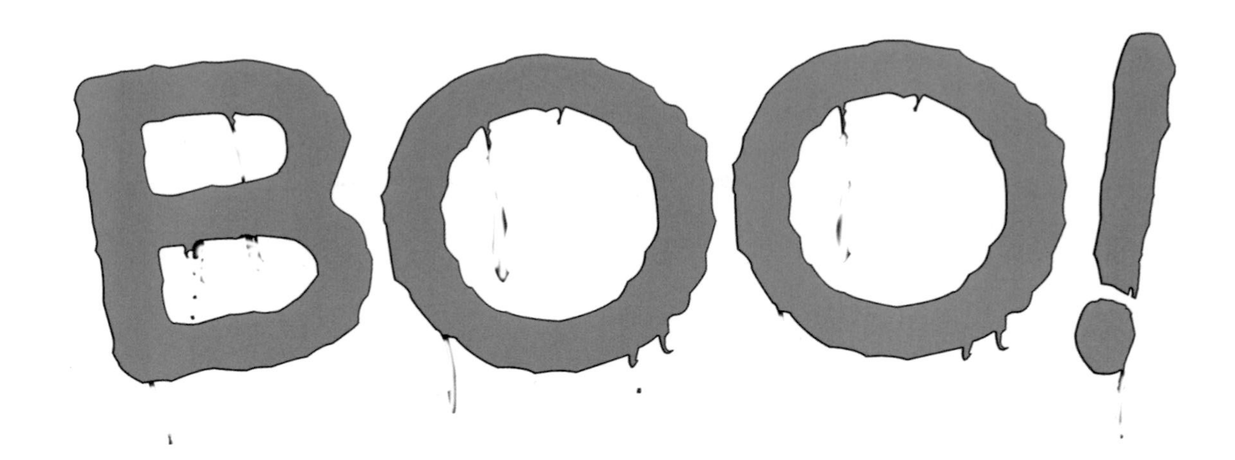

BOO!

ROBERT MUNSCH

ILLUSTRATED BY
MICHAEL MARTCHENKO

SCHOLASTIC CANADA LTD.
Toronto New York London Auckland Sydney
Mexico City New Delhi Hong Kong Buenos Aires

Scholastic Canada Ltd.
604 King Street West, Toronto, Ontario M5V 1E1, Canada

Scholastic Inc.
557 Broadway, New York, NY 10012, USA

Scholastic Australia Pty Limited
PO Box 579, Gosford, NSW 2250, Australia

Scholastic New Zealand Limited
Private Bag 94407, Botany, Manukau 2163, New Zealand

Scholastic Children's Books
1 London Bridge, London SE1 9BG, UK

www.scholastic.ca

The illustrations in this book were painted in watercolour on Crescent illustration board.

The type is set in 17 point Caxton Book.

National Library of Canada Cataloguing in Publication

Munsch, Robert N., 1945-
Boo! / Robert Munsch ; illustrations by Michael Martchenko
For ages 4-8.
ISBN 0-439-96126-2
I. Martchenko, Michael II. Title.
PS8576.U575B56 2004a jC813'.54 C2004-900448-4

ISBN-13 978-0-439-96126-4

30 29 28 27 Printed in China 62 23 24 25 26

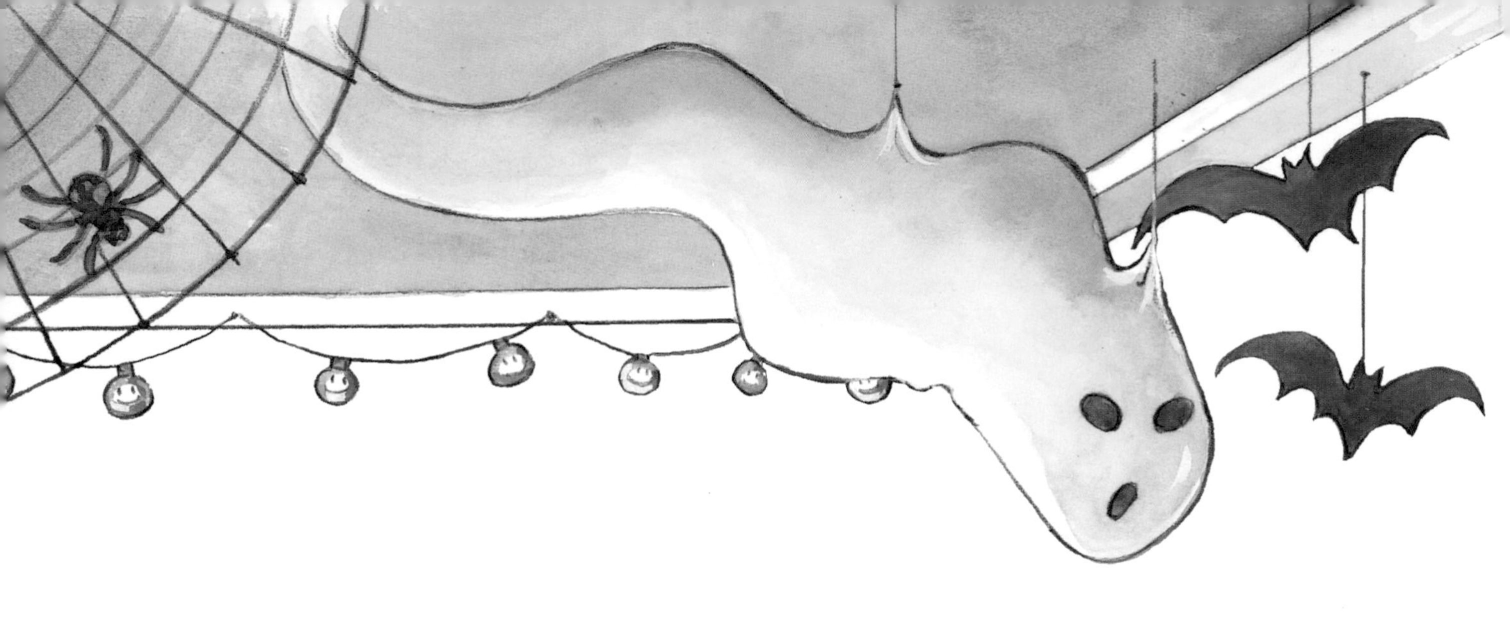

For Lance,
Hamilton, Ontario.
— R.M.

On Halloween, Lance went to his father and said, “This year, I am not going to wear a mask. I’m going to paint my face and make it very, very scary.”

“That’s nice, Lance,” said his father. “It’s a lot less work for me. You go and paint your face.”

So Lance went to the bathroom and painted:

worms coming out of his hair,
ants crawling on his cheeks,
and snakes coming out of his mouth.

Then he went downstairs, walked up behind his father, and said, "Boo!"

His father turned around and yelled,

"Ahhhhhhhhhhh!"

"Not scary enough!" said Lance. "I wanted him to fall over."

So Lance went back upstairs and painted:
green brains coming out the side of his head,
one eye falling down over his face,
and orange goop coming out of his nose.

Then he went downstairs, walked up behind his father, and said, "Boo!"

His father yelled,

"Ahhhhhhhhhhhh!"

and fell right over.

"Scary enough!" said Lance.

Then Lance put a pillowcase over his head, got another pillowcase for candy, and walked down the street.

He went up to a house:

KNOCK KNOCK KNOCK.

A big man opened the door and said, "First kid for Halloween! So nice to see a little kid for Halloween."

Lance lifted up his pillowcase and said, "Boo!"

The man yelled,

"Ahhhhhhhhhhh!"

and fell right over.

But Lance wanted some candy so he said very softly, "Trick or treat!"

Nothing happened.

He said it a little louder: "Trick or treat!"

Nothing happened.

So Lance went inside and there was an enormous table full of candy.

He put it ALL in his bag:

KAAAAA-*THUMP!*

Then, even though his bag was very heavy, he walked down the street and went to another house:

KNOCK KNOCK KNOCK.

A lady opened up the door and said, "First kid for Halloween! So nice to see a little kid for Halloween."

Lance lifted up the pillowcase and said, "Boo!"

The lady yelled,

"Ahhhhhhhhhhhh!"

and fell right over.

But Lance wanted some candy so he said very softly, "Trick or treat!"

Nothing happened.

He said it a little louder: "Trick or treat!"

Nothing happened.

So Lance went inside and there was an enormous table full of candy. He put it ALL in his bag.

KAAAAA-*THUMP!*

Then Lance went into the kitchen and opened up the refrigerator. He took out ten boxes of ice cream, twenty cans of ginger ale, three watermelons, ten frozen pizzas, and a turkey.

Lance dragged the pillowcase across the porch. He fell down the stairs and landed in the middle of the street.

A police car came by. The policeman jumped out, looked at Lance and said, "Kid, what's the matter with you? You can't sit in the middle of the street. Take your candy and go home."

"Look," said Lance, "my bag is so heavy I can't even move. I live right down the street. Please carry my bag home."

"Well, all right," said the policeman. "I'll take your bag of candy to your house . . . WHOA! IT'S A HEAVY BAG OF CANDY!"

The policeman dragged the bag down the street, put it on Lance's front porch, and said, "Kid! You must have gone to two thousand houses to get so much candy!"

"No," said Lance, "just two."

“Wait a minute,” said the policeman. “How did you get so much candy at just two houses?”

“Well,” said Lance, “my face is so scary, when people see it they fall over and I take all the candy in the house.”

“Hmm,” said the policeman. “I’m a cop. You can’t scare me. I want to see your face.”

“OK,” said Lance. He lifted up his pillowcase and said, “Boo!”

The policeman said, "Oh, if you think I'm going to fall over just because of a face like that, you are wrong. I'm going . . . I'm going . . . I'm going to . . . RUN AWAY!" And he jumped into his car and drove away really fast.

ZOOOOOOOOOOM!

Then Lance went inside and started to eat his first chocolate bar.

There was a knock on the door. Lance opened it and there was a teenager, the kind of kid who is much too old to go out for Halloween . . . and still goes out anyway!

He had a pillowcase over his head and a bag full of candy, much bigger than Lance's.

"Wow!" said Lance. "You must have gone to five thousand houses to get so much candy."

"No," said the teenager, "just five."

"How did you get so much candy at just five houses?" said Lance.

The teenager said, "My face is so scary that when people see it, they fall over, and I take all the candy in the house. And now I am going to scare *you* and take all the candy in *your* house."

"Maybe not!" said Lance. "I want to see your face."

"OK!" said the teenager. He lifted his pillowcase and yelled, "Boo!"

He had:

worms coming out of his hair,
butterflies coming out of his nose,
and ants coming out of his mouth.

He was scary, but not nearly as scary as Lance.

"Nice try," said Lance. He lifted his pillowcase and said,

BOO

The teenager yelled,

"Ahhhhhhhhhhhh!"

dropped his bag of candy, and ran down the street.

Lance took the teenager's bag of candy and dragged it into his house.

His candy lasted a long time. Every day, Lance ate as much as he could. He ate candy for breakfast, lunch, and dinner. He ate candy in the middle of the night. But his candy still lasted until . . .

NEXT HALLOWEEN!